A New Voyage
to the Country of the
HOUYHNHNMS

*Being the Fifth Part of the Travels into
Several Remote Parts of the World by*

LEMUEL GULLIVER

*First a Surgeon and then a Captain
of Several Ships*

Wherein the Author returns and finds a
New State of Liberal Horses and Revolting Yahoos

★

*From an unpublished manuscript
Edited, with notes, by*

Matthew Hodgart, M.A.

Sometime Fellow of Pembroke College, Cambridge

GERALD DUCKWORTH & CO LTD
3 Henrietta Street, London WC2
1969

First published in 1969 by
Gerald Duckworth & Company Limited,
3, Henrietta Street, London WC2

SBN 7156 05089

Printed in Great Britain by
Alden & Mowbray Ltd
at the Alden Press, Oxford

THE CONTENTS

INTRODUCTION

Y a singular stroke of good fortune, I discovered B the manuscript of this work during a visit to Dublin, Ireland, in September 1968. It was wrapped up in a bundle of filthy papers, in the attic of a crumbling eighteenth-century house. This house, situated in the Close of Saint Patrick's Cathedral, was about to be demolished (and has since been demolished) by the Dublin Corporation, and the papers were being removed from the premises by a rag-and-bone man, when I was able to identify the manuscript. Incontrovertible evidence concerning the handwriting and other matters, which I am publishing in a separate volume, shows it to be the work of Jonathan Swift; and it can be precisely dated to 1744, the last year of Swift's long and troubled life. This dating is of considerable biographical significance, since it has hitherto been believed that at this stage Swift had long been too insane to be capable of putting pen to paper, let alone of producing a work of even the slightest literary merit. That there are clear signs of insanity and senility in this work is beyond doubt: it is fragmentary, the narrative is not constructed with Swift's wonted smoothness and logic, and the style lacks the elegance and venom of his former genius. He also shows a tendency to

7

quote or allude to the *Fourth Part of* Gulliver's Travels, as if the educated reader were not entirely familiar with every word of that immortal, if distressing, work. Nevertheless I am confident that this text will be found to possess some historical value.

I was able to complete most of the fatiguing though delightful task of transcribing and editing the text in the calm surroundings of a great American university, where I spent the spring semester of 1969. Although many individual members of that university have made it possible for me to complete this work, I am reluctant to mention any names. Pending the publication of my full scholarly edition, I am offering this editio minor to the general reader, with a minimum of editorial apparatus. I have, however, felt that a few footnotes are necessary for the identification of accidental resemblances between the figments of Swift's diseased imagination and certain contemporary events. As the author puts it in "Verses on the Death of Dr. Swift":

> Yet, Malice never was his Aim;
> He lash'd the Vice, but spar'd the Name.
> No Individual could resent,
> Where Thousands equally were meant.

Ithaca, New York   M. H.
Brighton, Sussex
May–June 1969

A New Voyage to the
Country of the HOUYHNHNMS
&c.

CHAPTER ONE

Gulliver Undertakes a New Voyage

The Author's Disgust with his present Mode of Life. His Desire to Return to the Houyhnhnms. His Opinion as to the Whereabouts of Houyhnhnm-Land. His Literary Profits. A Fortunate Disclosure. Encounter with Pedro Mendez.

MY Reconcilement to the Yahoo-kind in general, which I hinted at the End of my last Book of Travels might at length prove possible, did not come about. At the end of a Year I could no longer permit my Wife or my Children to sit at Dinner with me, even though I kept my Nose well stopp'd with Rue, Lavender, or Tobacco-leaves, and I fell under a yet worse Apprehension of the Teeth and Claws of my neighbour Yahoos. I was tolerably happy only when sleeping in the Stable or conversing with my Horses for four Hours a Day. Yet at length even the Company of these amiable

Creatures failed to satisfy the intellectual Needs awakened in me by my curious Experiences on the various Islands, of which, gentle Reader, I have given thee a faithful History. My horses, though possessed of high moral Character and Sweetness of Disposition, could not (by Reason of their miserable Captivity in Yahoo-land) supply that Feast of noble Eloquence and wise Instruction, which I had in happier Days received from my Master and his Peers among the Houyhnhnms. My Visits to the Stables served only to stir in my Heart a Desire to return to the true Land of the Houyhnhnms, and once again to take part in calm and rational Discourse concerning the great Issues of Nature, Life and Art. I also wished (though I confess 'twas a less worthy Motive) to enjoy once more the comforting Solace of the humbler Sorrel Nag, who always loved me. I could not find any Rest, until I should once more, like *Ulysses* in his old Age, set out on an impossible Voyage.

Yet here I was faced with a fearful Dilemma. The Reader will recall that I had been banished from Houyhnhnm Land by an unanimous Vote of the Assembly, on these grounds: "because I had some Rudiments of Reason, added to the natural Pravity of those Animals, it was to be feared, I might be able to seduce them into the woody and mountainous Parts of the Country, and bring them in Troops by Night to destroy the Houyhnhnms' Cattle, as being naturally of the ravenous Kind, and averse from Labour." I have cited these solemn Words that the Reader may apprehend the Gravity of my Situation.

I had not been expelled by *Command*, but only by the Assembly's "hnhloayn" or *Exhortation*, for they have no Conception how a rational Being can be *compelled*, but only advised or exhorted. But I did not doubt for a Moment the Import of the Words; I knew that if I were ever again to be found trespassing on the Island, the Assembly would come to a swift Decision. Either they would politely but firmly kick me to Death, with a few terrible Yerks of their hinder Hooves; or (and this I feared as a Punishment infinitely more terrible) they would first remove the Rudiments of my Reason by a simple Operation with a sharp Flint, and then hand me over to a Band of Yahoos, by which I would soon be befouled, embraced and finally devoured. I pondered for some Days over these dreadful Alternatives, before I came to what I hoped was a rational Conclusion, worthy of my Education by my Master Horse. Rather than remain in England, tortured by restless Desires, I would return to the Horses' Island, and give myself up to the Assembly: I would plead guilty of Trespass, and accept the inevitable Consequences. But I would also humbly request the exquisite Pleasure of a few Days, or even Hours, spent for the last Time in rational Conversation, before Sentence was carried out. Then I should request the favour of Death by Kicking; or if my Offence in returning to the Island were judged too great for that humane Punishment and if Casting to the Yahoos were the only Sentence consonant with the Laws of Reason, then my final Request would be that I might be allowed to take my own Life. I felt sure that the

Houyhnhnms, as rational and kindly Beings, would not fail to grant these Pleas; and that accordingly, if my Plan succeeded, I could look forward to a few Moments of Happiness before departing from this wretched Life.

The desperate Undertaking I had resolved on was, however, no easy Matter, as the Reader will understand. First, I had to locate the Position of Houyhnhnm-Land on the Terrestrial Globe, which was by no means certain. As I related of my last Voyage, since my mutinous Crew had confined me to my Cabin, I had been unable to make Coelestial Observations, which would have given me the Latitude, nor had I in any Case a sufficiently accurate Chronometer to establish the Longitude; and when the Sailors put me ashore in the Long-Boat they told me with Oaths, whether true or false, that they knew not in what part of the World we were. However I did then believe us to be about ten degrees Southward of the Cape of Good Hope, or about 45 degrees Southern Latitude; and when I left the Island, I had resolved to steer my Course Eastward, hoping to reach the South-West Coast of *New-Holland*, to the South-East Point of which I eventually arrived. My successful Navigation had confirmed me in the Opinion, that I had long entertained, that the *Maps* and *Charts* place this Country at least three degrees more to East than it really is; which Thought I communicated many years ago to my worthy Friend Mr. Herman Moll,*

* Herman Moll: Dutch geographer and map-maker, who settled in London about 1698.

although he hath chosen to follow other Authors. I was therefore inclined to distrust Moll's Maps and to rely on my navigational Skill; and I hoped to find a Ship that would take me to or near to the same Point of New-Holland, whence I would proceed to the Houyhnhnms' Island in a well-equipped Long-Boat.

To find a Ship to undertake such a hazardous Voyage, on the Whim of a single Passenger, would, I believed, be excessively difficult; and so it turned out to be. The Cost of the Venture, the Reader may be surprised to learn, was no serious Obstacle. I had written a sober Account of my Travels, to soothe my lacerated Heart, and somewhat to my Astonishment this Book had been well received by the Publick. My Publisher, though belonging to that most scoundrelly sub-Tribe of the *English* Yahoos, who love to keep Authors and *Grub-Street* Hacks in Penury, had not been able to withold all the Profits from me; the work had been made into an Opera, which had played to crouded Houses at *Drury-Lane*; and it had also been translated into the *French* and divers other Tongues. From these Sources I had amassed a fairly large Sum of that Yellow Metal that the Houyhnhnms had taught me to despise, and while living frugally I invested it in sundry profitable Businesses. I was now moderately rich by Yahoo Standards, and was well able to support the Expense of a long Voyage, and even to buy for myself the Office of a *Super-cargo*.*

* *Super-cargo*: An officer on board a merchant ship whose business it is to superintend the cargo and the commercial transactions of the voyage.

I was not, however, rich enough to buy my own Ship, and to pay a Crew their Wages; and I must perforce find an Owner or a Captain willing to transport me to a remote Spot on the Globe, without my being able to reveal the true Reasons for such a Voyage; which Reasons, were I to reveal them, would scarcely be received as credible. I forced myself with Reluctance to approach some disgusting Sea-Yahoos at *Redriff*, *Portsmouth* and *Plymouth*, and broach the Proposition of a Voyage to New-Holland; but, as I had feared, they laughed in my Face (breathing forth as they did a Stench of Rum and Tobacco-juice).

After many months, heavy at Heart, I realised all my Capital in the Form of Gold and Promissory Notes, and took service as a Ship's Surgeon on a three-masted Schooner making for *Lisbon*. I hoped to meet again with Pedro de Mendez, the Portuguese Captain who rescued me at the end of my last Voyage, a very courteous and generous Person, and indeed the most civil Yahoo I have ever known. Now good Fortune came to my aid. A drunken Passenger confided to me in his Cups that he had discovered an immense Treasure, of a hitherto unknown Ore, at a point of New-Holland not many Leagues from the Coast where I had made Landfall. On my doubting his Claim, he showed me precise Maps and Charts, which made me certain that he was speaking the Truth as to the whereabouts of the Mine; he also showed me a Letter from an ingenious Chymist, a Member of the Royal Society, who had examined the Ore and pronounced that one day 'twould prove more precious than Gold.

Finding it was like to overblow, we took in our Sprit-sail, and stood by to hand the Fore-sail; but making foul weather, we looked the Guns were all fast, and handed the Missen. Despite these Precautions, my drunken Acquaintance was hit by a Boom and knocked overboard into the Bay of *Biscay*, where he perished. I lost no Time in taking Possession of his Papers, and now I was as happy as my general State of Mind would allow, for I had a real Inducement to offer to Mendez. If he were willing to command a Ship on this dangerous Voyage, he would be welcome to all the Profits that might accrue from the Mine of the new Ore; while I would be able to slip away quietly in a Long-boat for my last Trip on Earth. 'Twas a great Relief to me; for I had been unwilling to tell Mendez *the Thing that was not*, such was the Loathing for the horrible Practice of Lying that the Houyhnhnms had taught me.

My good Fortune held: after a few Weeks Mendez arrived in good Health from another Voyage. I excused myself from embracing him, on the pretext of a heavy Rheum, but we smiled at one another with Affection from the opposite Ends of a Tavern Room. It did not take me many Hours to convince him of the. . . .*

* Here follows a hiatus in the manuscript, where it has been eaten away by rats. It may safely be conjectured that the missing portion deals with Mendez's preparations for the voyage, various technical details of the voyage, Gulliver's leaving the ship off the coast of New Holland, and his setting out alone in his long-boat.

It should not, I think, be assumed that the narrative up to this point has any allegorical significance.

CHAPTER TWO

The New Yahoos

In the Long-Boat. Landfall. The New Yahoos. Their detestable Habits. Their publick Performances. Their colours of Hair. Their Sign-Talk. The Author escapes by Night. The Sorrel Nag.

WAS well provided for, in view of the uncertain Length of the Voyage I might have to undertake. My Boat had a small Sail, with which I could run before the prevailing Wind; and a pair of Oars. Stowed in a locker I had enough Ship's Biscuits and Water for several Weeks; and I carried on my Person my Pocket Perspective Glass and Pocket Compass, my Hanger* and Pistol; and in a waterproof Pouch a small Quantity of Powder and Shot and my Flint and Tinder Box. At first the Voyage went well, the Weather being temperate and the Sea tolerably calm: I considered that I was making good Speed for two and a half Days. Then I

* Hanger: a sword or cutlass.

was becalmed, and when I awoke on the next Morning I found myself in a thick Fog. Since I did not believe that there were any Reefs or other Hazards in the Vicinity I was not under any great Apprehension, but must remain for three days in a State of Impatience. Then towards the Evening I heard in the Distance a familiar Sound which caused me great Joy: it was the Whinnying of a Stallion. I could not make out the Words, but from the Tone I did not doubt but that it was a Master Horse giving Instructions to a Troop of Foals, as they carried out their daily Exercises. The Fog then began to clear and in the Light of the setting Sun I could see the wheeling Ranks break Formation and the several Foals plunge into a River for their daily cold Bath; in the Distance there were the neat and commodious wattle Houses of the Houyhnhnms, with a few of the Inhabitants sitting on their Hams before the front Doors. I began to row with the utmost Vigour, hoping to make a Landing at the nearest convenient Point; but to my Dismay a strong Current took me away from the Shoar. When I had ceased rowing in vain, I was out of Earshot. As darkness fell, the Current changed its Direction and ran parallel with the Shoar, so that my Boat drifted towards what I recollected as a wild and mountainous Region of the Island. I feared that, if I could not soon make a Landing, I should have a long Walk through Desart and Forest (with the Danger of encountering an occasional Band of Yahoos) before I might reach the inhabited Part of the Country; but since I could make no Headway against the Current and was by now considerably exhausted, I composed myself for Sleep.

I awoke just before first Light and saw to my Pleasure that I was now only a few hundred Yards from a rocky Shoar, where there seemed to be a possible Landing-place, by the Mouth of a River. I rowed to this Beach, and passed through the Surf without becoming swamped. Using driftwood Logs as Rollers, I pushed my Long-Boat up the shingle Beach above Highwater-Mark, and into the Mouth of a small Cave. I then fell on my Knees, and thanked Providence for my safe Return to the Island; consulting the notched Stick that served as my Calendar, I discovered that it was seven Years to the Day, since I had last set Foot on Houyhnhnmland. My Pleasure in Anticipation of meeting its rational Natives was clouded by the Thought, that I still had a long and possibly dangerous Journey before me. Since the Shoar ended in precipitous Cliffs on either Side, I must perforce go up the River into the Mountains and then strike across Country. Accordingly I shouldered my Knap-Sack, containing a few Provisions, and set off upstream, by a sort of natural Path, leading to a steep Gorge.

I had gone only a few hundred Yards into the Gorge, when I heard a distant Noise behind me. To my Horror I recognised the familiar growling and chattering of Yahoos; and climbing on a Boulder I saw through my Perspective Glass the first Specimens of the authentick Island-Yahoos that I had seen for seven Years, moving on all Fours in my Direction. In great Fear of the vile Creatures, I hastened up the

Gorge, which was becoming ever narrower; and with much Difficulty I traversed a foaming Waterfall and pressed on until I could hear their horrible Cries no longer. The Going was very difficult, but I could see that ahead the Gorge was widening out again. Arriving at a great Stone I peered over it, and saw to my Amazement an astonishing Sight, namely, a vast Concourse of Yahoos spread over a level Plain, the nearest of them being only a few Yards from my Stone. I was now like *a Rat in a Trap*; but after a Moment of Terror I saw that I had a Way of Escape, which was upwards. Glancing up, I noticed a narrow Fissure or *Chimney* in the Cliffs, which I might venture to climb. In my Youth I had acquired some Skill in the climbing of Rocks, and although now of a Middle Age I had kept myself in Trim by often ascending the Rigging on my Voyages. I was able to work myself slowly up the Chimney, crossing a dangerous Overhang without Mishap, until I reached a narrow Ledge some fifty feet above the River, and moved along it until I reached a shallow Recess. Here I reckoned I was tolerably secure: since I could not be reached from above, and if any of the Brutes climbed on to the Ledge I should be able to defend myself with my Hanger. I had completed my Climb not a moment too soon, since the Troop of Yahoos that had been following me up the Gorge at once passed beneath and joined the Throng in the open Plain. I greatly feared that they would smell me out, since I was sweating from my Efforts and from Terror; but I recollected to my Mortification that, since I was myself a Yahoo, I would smell no differently from the others, and would not be noticed. I need not however be seen by any of the Yahoos below me, since along the Ledge I found two Rocks with a Slit between them, whence I could observe the Scene in perfect Safety. But I needs must wait until Nightfall, before I might climb down, and make my way across the Plain and into the Mountains.

When I had composed myself, I applied my Pocket Perspective Glass to what lay before me. The Plain was grassy and roughly rectangular, and some of the Cliffs on its sides having the Appearance of ramparts, it distantly resembled (to my Fancy) a *Quadrangle* of some School or University; as for example the Great Court of *Trinity College, Cambridge* (at which University I had spent some years of my Youth), but having a much wilder Character. But infinitely more astonishing to me was the huge Throng of Yahoos. In the seven Years since I last saw them, their Numbers seemed to have increased beyond all Measure; since most were young Adults I conjectured that a prodigious Amount of Breeding must have taken place, even while I was last on the Island. I wondered greatly that so many were congregated on this Spot, and not usefully employ'd in the Fields and Pastures of the Houyhnhnms, many Miles away. But even more surprising was the bodily Appearance of these New Yahoos (as I must perforce call them). Their Hair, the Reader will recollect, had always been excessively long; but now it was even longer; when one of them occasionally came into a standing Position the Hair of the Head

22

would fall to below the Waist, while the pubic Hair swept down to the Knees. By Reason of this Abundance of Hair, I could not always distinguish the Gender of a Yahoo very clearly, as I had formerly been able to do by noting the long Dugs of the Females. That most if not all were infested with Vermin (probably the Head-, Body- and *Crab*-Louse) was evident from the continual Scratching of the affected Parts.

The outstanding Characteristick of the New Yahoos (and here, gentle Reader, I must change to the present Tense) is that they do greatly indulge in *Copulation*. As I observed from my Ledge on the first Occasion, and was later to receive many confirmatory Proofs, sexual Play taketh Place almost without Cease among them. Nor are they content with the traditional and natural Ways of copulating, whereby the Male jumps the Female, but they seek out a large Variety of Technicks for gratifying their Desires. In my previous Report, I perhaps erred in suggesting that unnatural Vice was an Invention of the Yahoos of *Europe*: for now the New Yahoos show every Aptitude at Carnal Deviation. Because of the Ambiguity of Gender, to which I have referred, it is usually impossible to state with Certitude whether the Catamitick or the Natural Mode is being practised; nevertheless they certainly manipulate every Member of the Body without Shame or Restraint, applying anything that is *Convex* to anything that is *Concave*. I shrink from further Description, even in the Obscurity of a learned Language; but conclude that their strenuous

Exertions tend to leave them in a State of perpetual Lassitude. From this Lassitude they try to rouse themselves by the taking of certain Herbs that have a Chymical Impulsion. In addition to the Root, very juicy, that I described in my last account, as producing the same Effect that *Wine* hath among us, they eat greatly of a Plant; which I was unable to identify on first Sight, but have subsequently ascertained to be a variety of *Cannabis indica*. The Effects of this Herb are obscure, beyond the manifest raising of a sweet, sickly Odour; but there can be no doubt that, although it may cause momentary Elation, it indisposeth most Yahoos to Labour, and aggravateth the detestable Vice of Idleness among them; while among a small Proportion of them it leads, by way of a *Crapula*, to sudden and irrational Rage, and sometimes to more deadly Appetites. Those, who have *graduated* from Cannabis, seek out a rare Mushroom, that hath the Property of causing Hallucinations. I have since been told by observant Houyhnhnms that some Yahoos after eating this Fungus take on an Appearance which we in England would describe as Visionary, Prophetick or Enthusiastick; the Houyhnhnms hold that the wretched Beasts have a temporary Illusion that they are rational Creatures, and even understand something about the World around them, or imagine that they are on a Voyage of Discovery. This Illusion does not, needless to say, persist, and the Subjects thereafter have their Faculties permanently impaired, their Brains (already highly imperfect) being now shot as full of Holes as a *Swiss* Cheese.

The New Yahoos have other Diversions besides eating dead Asses' Flesh, sleeping, copulating and partaking of narcotick Herbs, as I observed from the Cliff on the first day, and have received confirmation thereafter. They seem in Particular to be much gratified by a Sort of concerted Howling, which affordeth them infinite Relief. A small Group, of three, four or five Beasts, will crouch on a Mound, uttering Cries, which though they have no Melody, yet would seem to have a certain Rhythmick Principle, since the Executants will from Time to Time stamp on the Ground or beat with their Hands a hollow Log. The Response of the listening Yahoos varies between a cool Indifference (if it be possible to judge the Motions of the Brain from the Expression of their Muzzles) and a sort of painful Ecstasy: the younger Kind will let out Squalls and Screams, in a high-pitched Tone; which causes me to believe that these are usually of the *Female* Sex. At certain moments the whole Gathering will reform itself into Pairs, each whereof, shuffling about rapidly on all-fours, maketh in Concert gross movements resembling the obscœne and carnal Play of the Species: but whether these movements are made in Time with the Howling of the vocal Group, or no, I have been unable to determine. The Instinct for *Mimesis* or Imitation seems to be strong in these Animals, as it is with the Parrot or Dolphin, as appears in yet another of their Activities. Less frequently a rather larger Group or Troop will assemble on a Hillock, where they command the attention of the Throng, not so much by Howling and Stamping as by Chattering, Mopping and Mowing; at the same time they seem to be copying many of the Gestures used by Yahoos in the daily Business of Life, as Quarrelling, Guzzling, Vomiting, Excreting, Urinating, Cowering, Fauning, Creeping, and even those special Threatening Attitudes which I shall describe in their proper Place. Occasionally a Performer (if it may be called by that Name) will hold a Leaf to its Private Parts, so as to cover them imperfectly, and then cast it away with an Expression of roguish pleasure; although why this affords Gratification to a naked Animal I cannot understand. Whether these Series of Actions do in fact represent a kind of dramatick Performance, hitherto unparalleled among the lower Orders of Creation, I will not venture to pronounce; my tentative Belief that this might indeed be the case was shaken, when I noted that the principal Activities represented by Gestures were none other than the usual Yahoo Modes of Masturbation and Copulation; and that very often the Performers would leave their Hillock to join the watching Throng, where they would continue the same Activities in indiscriminate Partnership with the Spectators; or they would make aggressive Gestures at the Spectators, until the latter were persuaded to run up to the Hillock and themselves indulge in Pantomime. I may be censured by captious Criticks for even daring to mention the *Hypothesis*, that these Actions have anything to do with the Play-House; but I consider it the duty of the Traveller to make cautious Speculation, as well as exact Observation.

I will not risk my Reputation for Truthfulness, by suggesting that any of the *other* Activities, that I have witnessed among the Yahoos, bear any remote Analogy to the Arts. For example, one Yahoo takes a smooth stone from the slaty *Strata* of the Cliffs, and, laying it on the Ground, smears it with a Mixture of Excrement and red Ochreous Ore, sometimes in a pattern of irregular Lines but more often in random Streaks; and the Result he contemplates lovingly. Another heaps up little Mounds of Pebbles or of Earth, whereon he may place Tufts of Grass or Twigs. Yet another makes a collection of Turds, which are evidently chosen for their significant Forms, and arranges them carefully in Niches of the Rocks. I have noted that the Excrements of the Houyhnhnms (doubtless stolen furtively from the Stables) are especially prized, perhaps because of their elegantly squarish Shape. A passing Yahoo will pause briefly before one of these Slates or Mounds, and, cocking his Head to one side and opening his Mouth, will stare at it in Wonder, before scratching himself and shambling slowly off.*

Before I describe the most striking Behaviour of the New Yahoos I must amplify some Observations that I made in the Account of my last Voyage. I noted that their Heads and Breasts are covered with a thick Hair, some frizzled and others lank; and that the Hairs of both Sexes were of several Colours, brown, red, black and yellow; while their Skins were

* Two exhibitions were held at Cornell University and elsewhere in the United States in the spring of 1969, one of "Earth Art", the other of "Soft and Semi-soft Sculpture".

all of a brown Buff colour. I observed that the Red-haired of both Sexes were more libidinous and mischievous than the rest, whom yet they much exceeded in Strength and Agility. After my Observations on the first Day, and later Discussions with judicious Houyhnhnms, I can now state that there are other important Differences connected with these Colours of Hair. The Red-haired, for instance, are of a superiour physique, braver, more cleanly in their Habits, softer in Voice, and more restrain'd in their Behaviour; on the other Hand, they appear to have a greater Capacity for Violence. The others are infinitely more Revolting in their Appetites, and more given to cowardly Whining and Tantrums.*

The Yahoos have no Language, in the strict Sense of the Word, which implies meaningful Discourse by means of the Voice; they can only grunt, howl or squeak; yet they have a plentiful Variety of Gestures, which from careful Study can be discovered to bear some Significance. (The same hath been lately reported of the *Chimpanzees* of the Africk forests.) Most of these Gestures are simply obscœne, consisting as they do of groping at their private Organs or miming sexual Actions; but they can also communicate by pointing at their Mouths or Bellies, and at Objects they require, such as Asses' Flesh. The Houyhnhnms have always understood the Sign-Talk of the Yahoos tolerably well, and by

* This remark, in which Swift establishes a clear preference for the red-haired over the other varieties of Yahoo, would possibly be stigmatised today as "racist". Red hair is common enough among the Celtic peoples: could it be that Swift, an Irishman, intended yet another insult to Ireland?

the Light of Nature the Yahoos clearly understand some of the Houyhnhnms', as when by an imperious Shake of the Hoof they issue a Command, or threaten Punishment to Malefactors. On the first day of my Return, however, I observed several new Gestures among the Yahoo Throng, or at least some that had escaped my View on my previous Visit. These were used only by a Small Minority; since the great Part of the Throng were evidently content with their traditional Postures and Moppings. First, each of a small Band would clench his Fist, and acting in Concert with the rest, would raise it to the Level of his Forehead, with the Elbow bent. What this meant I could not determine, unless it served to demonstrate the Cohesion or Solidity of the Group. Secondly, they would extend both Arms, with the Wrists bent back and the Palms open; this was followed by a forceful upwards and forwards Movement, as if they were trying to push someone or something up against a Wall—but that is only a Conjecture. They would make these Signs before making short Rushes in Unison, always towards the same Point of the Compass, which on Reflection I saw to be the Direction of the Houyhnhnms' Habitations. At the End of each Rush, they would glare in that Direction, shaking their Fists and making the usual filthy Signs. I did not at that Time at all understand the Meaning of these Acts. To my surprise I saw a large Brute tear off a Branch from a Tree and wave it in the Air, as if it were some Weapon; for such a Thing I had not seen on my last Visit; at this Time I put it down to Chance.

Later in the Day these active Bands withdrew to remoter Parts of the Valley, where they seemed to have Caches hidden in Caves and Thickets; but what was contained therein I could not ascertain, even with my Perspective Glass.

The After-Noon Sun became insupportably hot. Wearied by my Toils of the Morning, and expecting a laborious Walk throughout the Night, I tried to sleep; but could not, by Reason of the continual Chattering and Howling from the huge Throng below me. Also my Nose was assailed by the intolerable Stench that rose from the Multitude. After witnessing an especially disgusting Orgy, in which a Band of six or seven were taking part (the Details whereof I shrink from mentioning, even in a philosophical Treatise), I fell a-Vomiting, which afforded me much Relief. As the Sun set a Sea-wind arose and I felt easier: the Noise and the Smell grew somewhat less; I dozed for a short Space, then ate of my Ship's Biscuits and drank from my Water-Bottle. When it had been quite dark for two Hours and the Throng had fallen silent, I climbed slowly along the Ledge and down the Cliff, and moved circumspectly across the Valley, to a Point where I believed there was an Exit into the Forest. Holding my Nose, I passed between Heaps of slumbering Yahoos; once I stumbled over the Feet of one, and drew my Hanger in great Fear. But the Brute was sunk in a drugged Stupour and did not wake.

At length I found a Crevice, whence I could leave the Valley; and after an easy Climb, entered a wild Forest. I had no longer any Fear of meeting a stray

Band of Yahoos, and I knew that the Island was not infested by any other Species of dangerous Animal. Using my Pocket-Compass by the Light of a waning Moon, I struck out in the direction of the Houyhn-hnms' Fields and Houses; and it was not many Hours before I reached the first Plot of cultivated Land. As I reckoned that it was still some Time until Dawn, I rested in a Thicket as best I could. When I awoke, I had recovered from my horrible Experience of the Yahoo Throng; and was conscious only of my Will and Duty, which was to give myself up to my Houyhnhnm Master as soon as possible. I washed myself in a Stream and made my Appearance as neat as I could, then walked across the Meadows towards a Hut on the Horizon. I had not gone over a Quarter of a Mile, before I saw a Horse trotting over the Brow of a Hill in the middle Distance; doubtless, I thought, one of the humbler Sort, out at this early Hour to overlook the work of the Field-Yahoos (though of the latter I could see none). When the Horse saw the Form of a standing Yahoo, he galloped up with great Speed to investigate; and in a few seconds I recognised, in a Transport of Joy, the Lineaments of my old Friend, the Sorrel Nag. I shouted to him in his Language, "The Gentle Yahoo has come back!" and then overcome by my Emotion, hurled myself to the Ground before his advancing Hooves. In broken whinnyings I sobbed out, "I am back, I have come to give myself up. Take me to our Master, entreat him to grant me one hour of rational Discourse, then let me suffer the sentence of the Assembly ..." The Sorrel Nag stopped before me in Silence; when I looked up, I saw that he too was weeping. Then he replied, in his pleasant rustick Brogue, "Trouble thyself not, gentle Yahoo, about such matters. Nor needst thou fear the Exhortations of the Assembly: things are different now. Welcome back!"

CHAPTER THREE

The Roan's History

Changes among the Houyhnhnms. The Author learns how these came about. His own Part in them. The Yahoos' "Demand". They occupy a Stable, and are ousted by Bulls. The Consequences thereof.

PICKED myself up, and embraced the Nag tenderly; and then walked towards the Village beside him. After a few minutes, he informed me that my old Master was dead, which caused me great Dismay: he added that there was a new Master now, but did not volunteer any Particulars. There were many things I wished to ask him about: in what respects were Things different now; why were there so few Yahoos working in the Fields, for I could see but a few decrepit white-haired Brutes dragging a harrow; and above all, why I need not fear the Assembly's Exhortations. But I remembered that the Sorrel Nag, though the

c

most amiable Soul in existence, was not gifted with philosophical skill; so I determined to leave my questioning until I might address a more erudite Horse. As we approached the Village, a Number of Houyhnhnms, struck by the unwonted Sight, came galloping out to meet us. I recognized a few familiar Countenances. First there was the Dapple-Grey Charger, now no longer young, who came of a Clan reckoned to be the noblest on the Island and the best endowed with Strength and Integrity. When he recognized me, he snorted and turned away indignantly, showing his Resentment at the Spectacle of an outlaw'd Yahoo, as I believed he had every Right to do. Next, there were a Troop of Houyhnhnms, of the Middle Age and the Middle Station in Life, whom I had known well on my last Visit; these greeted me, with some Warmth tinged with Embarrassment; they looked as if they had something to hide, an Expression I had never seen on the Face of a Houyhnhnm; and they were also in less excellent Condition than I remembered. Lastly, there were very many of the younger Generation, Colts and Twenty yearlings, who crouded around me in silent Wonder, which soon changed to positive Enthusiasm, though from what Cause I did not then know. I could hear the Exclamation "New Yahoo!" spoken among them, even after the Word had gone round that I was none other than the old Yahoo who had appeared on the Island before they were grownup. I was struck by the Appearance of some of these Youths: they were remarkably unkempt, and did not sport the glossy Coats and trim Fetlocks, that

34

Houyhnhnm Convention once demanded, and disciplined Exercise produced. A few even had Manes so shaggy, that they would distantly have reminded me of Yahoos' Hair, had I not banished such an Absurdity from my Mind. Others carried Burrs and Clots of Dirt on their Legs, whereof the accustomed self-grooming should have rid them. But in the Stir of my Arrival I had no Opportunity of further observing them.

I was graciously entreated to enter the Hut of my good Friend, the Roan, and there was set before me a Dish of boiled Oats and Milk, which did much refresh my weary Spirits. After I had eaten and rested for a while, I entreated my gracious Host, that he would grant me the Honour of a Conversation; which he was clearly eager to do. I then explained the Reasons why I had come back to the Island, after enduring great Straits in the Voyage; stated my Intention of giving myself up as an Outlaw; and openly mooted the Questions, that I had pondered during my Meeting with the Sorrel Nag, in particular why he should have said that I had no longer anything to fear from the Exhortations of the Assembly and that Things were now different. His Honour replied, after the customary Deliberation of his People, that the Sorrel Nag had spoken the Truth, incapable as he was of saying *the Thing that was not*; that there was indeed a New Spirit abroad among the Houyhnhnm Race, adding with a Metaphor, doubtless drawn from one of their famous antient Poems, that "the winds of Change were blowing". That in Truth I had nothing to fear from the General

Assembly, who would certainly pardon my Transgression against their former *Exhortation*; and in fact a Committee of that Assembly had already asked him to convey this Message privately to me. When I expressed my Regret at the untimely Death of my former Master, and asked that my Condolences be expressed to his surviving Family, he replied that the Master had died not many Months after I had left the Island, in strange Circumstances. As the Reader will recollect from my former Account,* Houyhnhnms usually die at the Age of Seventy or Seventy-five Years, in the utmost Composure, taking "a solemn Leave of their Friends, as if they were going to some remote Part of the Country, where they designed to pass the rest of their Lives". This was by no means the case with my late Master. He expired in his ripe Maturity, of some wholly obscure Disorder; and just before his Death, he showed great Perturbation of the Spirits, crying out (as the Bystanders remembered) "I see ... Anarchy ... Chaos ... Fire ... Blood..."; but how such Disasters could affect the peaceful and prosperous Œconomy of Houyhnhnm-Land no one at that Time could imagine. A new Master had taken his Place in the Family, and soon afterwards this noble Horse had, by the unanimous Vote of the Assembly, assumed the general Governance, and was now Master of the whole Island. I reflected that this was a System of Government more suited to Lilliput or Brobdingnag than to the time-honoured Ways of this Land; but of the Character of this Ruler I learned

* *Gulliver's Travels*, Part IV, ch. 9.

36

little more during this Colloquy. I next gave a brief Account of my dreadful Experiences among the Yahoos on the previous Day; and also expressed my Wonder that so few Yahoos were visibly working on the Land, while so many were lying in beastly Idleness up-Country. My Host, heaving a deep Sigh, said that he could not forbear to tell me the whole Truth, and embarqued on a long History, of which the following is a Summary.

"The troubles of our Country," (he said) "gentle Yahoo, began with you." When I started in Dismay, he added courteously: "Do not think that I wish to blame you; since it was not your Fault that you were carried here. But your Presence was a disturbing Influence. The first Debate ever held at the General Assembly took place on your Account, on the Question (subsequently decided in the Negative), Whether the Yahoos should be exterminated from the Face of the Earth. The Motion to expel you from the Island, as a potentially dangerous Animal (a Yahoo endowed with a Modicum of Reason) was passed without Opposition; but, after you had gone, many of us fell into a State of Doubt. Since you had shown yourself as free from Malice and Untruthfulness, and were in many ways an amiable, nay benevolent, Creature, could it be that *all* Yahoos were wholly evil? True, you had given us no very favourable Account of your Countrymen, which confirmed many in their Belief that all Yahoos were essentially base, but the Memory of your admirable Character continued to disturb our Thoughts. We began to question our pre-conceived View of the

37

Yahoos" (I did not wholly understand this Phrase). "Was not, perhaps, their Vileness caused by the fact that we had exploited them cruelly, as, for example, by forcing them to *work*? Could we not expect some Change of Heart in the Brutes if we were to adopt a more liberal Policy towards them? The debates swayed this way and that, without coming to any clear Conclusion; and meanwhile the old Way of Life went on much as before.

"During the Harvest Season of the following Year, we were distressed by the increasing Idleness of the Farm-Yahoos. The Corn was plentiful, and we had much Trouble in getting it in before the Rains of the Autumnal Equinox, for many of the Brutes would lie down and go to sleep, when they should have been dragging Sledges. We had long been used to their dumb Insolence, which had always been swiftly punished, but now some of our Overseers seemed to find the Beasts less tractable than before, or could not bring themselves to apply the usual Discipline. To the surprise of one Overseer, a small Gang of the most deformed Creatures left their Work, and coming up to him, made a *Demand*. Now, just as there is no word for *Command* in our Language but only one for *Exhortation* (for we do not understand how a Rational Being can fail to obey the Dictates of Reason), so there is no Word for *Demand*: a Houyhnhnm who desires a Service from another will make a *Request*, and if the Request is reasonable, as it nearly always is, it will not fail to be granted. The word *Demand* must therefore be expressed in Paraphrase by us; and by the Yahoos, as on that first Occasion, by a new Set of Gesticulations, that were then outside the usual Range of their Sign-Talk. It was in Consequence difficult for the Overseer and for the other Houyhnhnms that he consulted to make out just what the Yahoos were *demanding*. But from their Pantomime we gathered that they desired not only to rest for the remainder of the Moon, but also in Future to work only at the Times, and in the Manner that they saw fit. This Demand was indignantly refused, and the Overseer was about to apply the traditional Remedy for Idleness, and for other Diseases contracted by Greediness and Repletion,* when the Gang ran with great Speed into a Coppice and thence into the Forest, before the Overseer could apprehend them. It was believed that they had gone to join the wild Yahoos in the Mountains, whose Numbers, our Scouts had reported, had of late prodigiously increased. There were several other Incidents of the same kind in the next Moons; and, more alarming, there were a growing number of Raids made by the Mountain-Yahoos on our Asses and Cattle. The Brutes were showing greater Boldness and Cunning in their almost nightly Thefts of our Goods; and sometimes they would mutilate an Ass, or break down a Fence, not for any Profit to themselves, but merely, it seemed, for the Pleasure of Destroying.

"In the following Spring, during the Season of Sowing, a small Group of Yahoos suddenly ran in

* *Gulliver's Travels*, Part IV, ch. 7: "the Cure prescribed is a Mixture of *their own Dung* and *Urine*, forcibly put down the *Yahoo's* Throat".

39

from the Fields, and entered the principal Stables. They were joined by a few who had come down from the Mountains, and hidden overnight nearby; and among them were recognised some of the deformed Creatures, that had escaped the Year before. Together they drove out a few Foals and young Mares, that were feeding in the Stables; and with unheard-of Ingenuity barricadoed the Doors, behind which they set up a terrible Yowling. We were so taken aback that we failed to act with Swiftness and Resolution; after a while we attempted to force the Doors open, but by then it was apparent that we could not do so without suffering some Damage to our Persons and Property, so firmly had the Brutes fortify'd themselves. We then made our first great Error: for we held a special Meeting of the Assembly, and debated the Situation. Some were for instant Action, without regard to the now considerable Dangers involved: they argued that this was a Plot of only a Small Minority of the Field-Yahoos, since the greater Bulk of them were still working peaceably at their Tasks, whether from Fear of Discipline or (as was more likely) from Force of Habit. Others proposed that the Assembly should at least find out what the insurgent Yahoos *demanded*, before taking any irrevocable Action; and the latter carried the Day. Accordingly we waited until a Leader of the Group should make himself visible; which one soon did by climbing up a Chimney and exhibiting himself on the Roof of the Stables. There he performed the same Pantomime, though mingled with more obscœne Gestures, that we had seen last Year, and was understood to be making the same Demands as before: *viz.* for working only on the Yahoos' own terms. We went back to the Assembly, where this Demand was agreed to be unacceptable to the Majority of us; but it remained to be debated what sort of Action, if any, should be taken."

My friend then reminded me of a Fact that I had failed to mention in my Relation of my last Voyage; namely, that the Houyhnhnms possess not only Asses and Milch-Cows (though no Pigs) but a Herd of savage *BULLS*. These Bulls, with their great Humps of Muscle and long sharp Horns, are the most dangerous of living Creatures: they will not hesitate to attack any other Thing that moves. This Quality of Ferocity hath been produced by careful Breeding, as with the fighting Bulls of *Miura*, in the Kingdom of Spain; and like the Spanish Bulls, they can be controul'd by the judicious Use of Steers and other like Skills of Herdmanship, wherein the Houyhnhnms are adept. The Herd was kept in Reserve for any grave Emergency that might arise; as, for Instance, an Invasion of Yahoos from Overseas (which since my last Visit had seemed to the more prudent to be at least a Possibility). The Assembly, by the Vote of the Majority, now determined to use these Bulls, to oust the Yahoos from the Stables. Accordingly, the Herd was brought up to the Stables, and turned loose; and in a few moments the Bulls had smashed down the Doors and Barricadoes with their Horns, and evicted the Occupants, not without tossing and goring a few

Individuals. Most of the Yahoos, however, escaped without much Hurt, thanks to their prodigious Nimbleness, that enabled them to Somersault over the Bulls' Horns and run off to the Woods. We rapidly brought the Bulls under Controul, and herded them back to their Corral, and then went inside the Stables to inspect the Damage. To our Horrour, we found that the Yahoos had broken every Manger and every Flint and Wooden Tool that they could lay their Hands on, and had left the Stables in total Disorder. They had also deposited their Excrements in extream amounts all over the Hay and the Floors.* Even more disgusting was the Report from a Herding Horse that the Female Yahoos of the Gang had stanch'd their Menstrual Flow with Hay and Leaves, which they flung at the advancing Bulls, a Thing utterly abhorrent to Nature; whereof we found revolting Tokens on the Floor.†

When we returned from our Inspection, we saw another remarkable Sight. Most of the Field-Yahoos, who had hitherto shewn little Interest in the Events at the Stables, had struck off work, and were either crouching sullenly beside their Harrows, or were stumbling off the Woods on the trail of the escaped Occupiers. It was difficult to determine the Motives for their Actions: some Houyhnhnms alledged that it was Fellow-feeling for those of their Tribe who had

* A similar incident has been credibly reported at the University of California, Berkeley Campus.

† The equivalent was reported from Columbia University, New York, Spring 1969.

been smartly treated by the Bulls; others, that they were merely seizing the temporary Commotion among their Masters as an Opportunity to indulge their natural Idleness and Insubordination. Be that as it may, we have since been unable to persuade many of the Brutes to return to their wonted Tasks, to this very Day. As you have seen, some of the older Yahoos still continue to labour in the Fields; but the Bulk have gradually dispersed to the Woods and Mountains, where we fear they are plotting some new Mischief.

"The Condition of the Stables, after the Yahoos had left, was such as to make them unfit for further Habitation. Accordingly, we decided to burn them down and build them anew, with fresh Stakes and Wattle. And (although the Term is Yahoo-like, and would not formerly have been considered consonant with the Decorum of our Traditions) we agreed to commemorate that Day, the saddest in our Annals, as the *Great Shit-In*."

CHAPTER FOUR

The Chestnut: Modes of Liberal Instruction

Barbarous new Terms. The Chestnut excuses the present Depravity of the Yahoos. Projects for their Reformation. New Modes of instructing the Houyhnhnm Youth. The Author expounds the Systems of Instruction in Europe. The Chestnut's dithyrambick Enthusiasm. The Advancement of Crime in Europe and America. The Yahoos' Demand. The New Master's liberal Speech. The Debate adjourned.

I LISTENED to the Roan's History with Attention and growing Disquiet; and when he had ended I put some Questions to him on points that still remained obscure. I wished to understand how it was that the rational Houyhnhnms could ever have allowed such Things to happen; to ascertain the various Shades of Opinion among which they were now divided, especially those of the Younger Sort; and to investigate the Motives of

hardest. All Yahoos had been born free, and now were everywhere in Chains; or rather (he corrected himself) they were so until recently, when they had shown some Inclination to improve their Conditions of Life. When I objected that this View of the Yahoos' Nature did not agree with my Observations of the wild Creatures which I had seen in the Mountains, he replied, that I, the gentle Yahoo, clearly did not understand their rough Island Ways, being used as I was to the greater Corruption of the *European* Tribe of Yahoos; which he remembered my describing at length on my previous Visit. What I had now depicted as disgusting orgies (he said) was no more than the brisk Intemperance of Youth, which must have its Fling of the Hoof or Paw. When I had talked of the destructive Ferocity of the more *Active* Yahoos, I had been understandably prone to exaggerate: what I had seen was but a harmless Mode of shewing their Impatience with the Present State of Affairs. Their *Concern* to better the wretched Lot of their Fellow-Creatures had something commendable about it, though sometimes he deplored the Means they employed. They might be Savages, he thought, but they were Noble Savages. I did not understand his Meaning, and changed the Topic of Discourse.

How did he and his Friends propose, I inquired, to get the Field-Yahoos back to Work before the next Harvest; and how to make the wilder Ones cease from raiding their Stockades and carrying off their Asses? "By Education," he replied. "Ah Education, delightful Task, to rear the tender

47

Thought, to teach the young Idea how to shoot."* They should win over all the Yahoos gradually by implanting the Seeds of Virtue in their Minds; by improving their Gesture-Language until it become more expressive; and in Time by moulding their imperfect vocal Soundings into the true Houyhnhnm Speech, which was the Vehicle of Reason and the Medium of Art. Did the Chestnut mean that he would expose the Yahoos to the traditional Education of the Houyhnhnm Youth, which consisted of the disciplined Acquisition of Skill in Poetry and in Athletic Feats? "No, not precisely that," he replied, "for we have of late made Changes in the Upbringing of our own Youth. Some few Teachers still insist on the daily Training of the Canter on the Downs, and the Plunge into the Cold River, and the Study of the antient Odes; but many of us have come to feel that this is too circumscribed a Way of imparting Knowledge and Skill, and doth not sufficiently allow the Soul of a Young Horse to sprout like a Grain of Oat. Instead we encourage the Young to Study the Constitution of the Society wherein they live (with a View to altering it) and also the vital Workings of the Yahoo Community. We do indeed reward them for composing Poetry, but we are not scrupulous in requiring that they use the Prosody and Style of our traditional Verse; if they should wish to chuse a freer Form of Verse (or no Form at all) to express their Feelings, so much the

* James Thomson, *The Seasons* (1728), "Spring", lines 1152-3. It has not previously been known that Swift was familiar with the verse of James Thomson.

better. And as for taking Athletic Exercise and Bathing, we leave it to our young People to decide whether they will or no. I would banish all the old Tales and Epics of our Ancestors from the Curriculum, save one—the Tale of the Abandoned Horse, all alone on a little Island, how he learned first to follow Nature and thereby to discover for himself all the primal Virtues.* Above all we must *Permit* them to develop all their Capacities without Let or Hindrance; and in this the Yahoos do set us a good Example, in the liberal Treatment which they give their Brats. Kindness is all, for what Wisdom do you find that is greater than Kindness? It is this new and improved System of Education that we wish to apply to the Reclamation of the Yahoo Kind, and we doubt not but that it will be wholly beneficial."

The Chestnut asked me whether I had any Views on this great Matter of Educating the Young. I said that I could only speak from my own Experience. My Father had sent me, at the Age of fourteen to *Emanuel-College* in *Cambridge*, where I had resided three years; but the Charge of maintaining me being too great for his narrow Fortune, I had left to study Physick; I was first bound Apprentice to a Surgeon for four Years, and then studied at *Leyden* for two Years and seven Months. At *Cambridge* and at the other University of England, although there were some poor Boys in my Case, who applied themselves

---

* A curious anticipation of Jean-Jacques Rousseau's *Emile* (1762), where it is said that all books should be banished from the educative process, with the exception of *Robinson Crusoe* (1719–20) by Daniel Defoe. With the latter, of course, Swift was familiar.

close to their Studies, the leading Students were
young Noblemen and Gentlemen, who lived in
Idleness and Luxury; and spent their Time in
Drinking, Whoring, Cock-fighting, Gambling, play-
ing Billiards, smashing Glass and other gallant
Pursuits, which I was at Pains to interpret. Their
Minds were Compositions of Spleen, Dulness,
Ignorance, Caprice, Sensuality and Pride. The
Teachers, or Fellows, in whose Care they were,
neglected their Duties, and passed their Days in a
Torpor, induced by Repletion and Portugal-juice.
In consequence, little Study of Poetry, of the
Principles of Agriculture, or of other Useful Arts,
took Place in the Universities; and in my Time
Learning was advanc'd by the more practical Yahoos
of the Market-Place. In contrast to the illiberal,
though usually peaceful, Seminaries of *England*, the
Schools of the Continent of *Europe* presented a
Scene of lively Activity. The Students' Hands were
often on their Swords, drawing Blood in Brawls
among themselves, or in Outbreaks against the
Yahoos of the Towns, whose high Prices for Food
and Lodging they were forced to pay. The Yahoos of
the Gown (a black Cloth worn as a distinguishing
Mark) resented the Avarice and Ignorance of the
Town; while the Town considered the Students to be
turbulent and arrogant; and so they would lash out
and lash back at each other. I considered that there
was little to chuse between the Systems of England
and of Europe. In both I had observed that the
greater Bulk of the Scholars were by Nature indisposed to Toil; and that, if they were compelled

to pass rigourous Tests, to prove their Possession of Knowledge, and if they failed in these Tests, they would often raise their Hands in Anger, against the Persons of their Professors. On the other Hand, if they were not so tested (as was the Case with our English Lords), they learned nothing of Use to themselves or to their Neighbours.

Wearying of the Topick of Education, I asked if they had sanguine Expectations of a Reconcilement with the Yahoos, and of the future Peace and Prosperity of the Island. The Chestnut replied that he was wholly confident in the Progress of the Œconomy; that there would be hard Days ahead, he thought, but he was certain that Reason and Liberal Sentiment would prevail in the End. Nay more, there was a great Day about to Dawn, in which Yahoo and Houyhnhnm would walk together, Hoof in Paw, through the Meadows of Communal Joy. It would soon be apparent that our present Sufferings were illusory, our present Evils providential; we were safe in the Hand of one disposing Power, Or in the Mortal or the Natal Hour; whatever was, was Right.* If it were objected that the Yahoos' Appetites were excessive, then he would reply that the Road of Excess led to the Stables of Wisdom; if some said that the Brutes were violent and angry, he would tell them (and now the big round Tears ran down his dappled Face)† that the Yahoos of Wrath

* Swift is here quoting from *An Essay on Man* (1733–4) by his friend Alexander Pope.

† "The big round tears run down his dappled face." James Thomson, *The Seasons* (1730), "Autumn", line 454.

were wiser than the Horses of Instruction. He concluded by saying that he saw a shining Vision of the Future, a new Sky and a new Earth, which would be peopled by a new and glorious Race of Beings, the Horse-Yahoos!

After the Chestnut had reached the dithyrambick Conclusion of his Speech, which embarrassed even some of his Friends, there followed the Moment of Silence, customary in Houyhnhnm Conversation. Then another present (whose Name I do not remember) said: "Gentle Yahoo, we have been talking much of the Affairs of our Island; but now wilt thou be good enough, we entreat thee, to tell us something more of the Yahoo Kingdoms of Europe, whereof we have heard nothing for seven years?"

I replied that in seven Years there had been no great changes in the Affairs of Europe, proceeding as they do from the corrupted Institutions and base Hearts of its Inhabitants. Our History continueth to be little more than the Register of the Crimes, Follies and Misfortunes of Yahoo-Kind, or a Chronicle of Wars, Revolutions, Conspiracies, Ryots, Frauds, Bankruptcies, Orgies and Frivolities. But if there is one Subject that doth oppress my Spirits more than another, it is the great increase of Crime among us, and especially in our *American* Plantations; and since you kindly ask me to speak, I will speak on that Head. Crime hath lately increased so much in the City of *London*, that a Citizen cannot walk in the Streets by Night or by Day without Fear of Foot-pads, who may hit him on the Head and run off with his Watch and Yellow

Metal. A traveller can scarce cross the great Heath that lyeth to the North of *London* without a Yahoo mounted on a Houyhnhnm presenting a deadly Tube at him, and demanding, not without some Show of Civility, his Purse. The Young have formed themselves into disorderly Bands, calling themselves *Mohocks* after a Tribe of *American* Yahoos, for the Purpose of beating elderly Males, rowling elderly Females in Tubs, and other like Tokens of Gallantry; or *Nickers*, whose Pleasure it is, when drunk, to break Windows with small Coins. The Mob of baser Yahoos is ever ready to ryot with Brickbats in defence of License and for the Persecution of religious Sects. To combat these and other Dangers to Life and Limb, we have Laws, Juries, Magistrates and Constables (and here I gave a simple Explanation of these Terms). The Laws are severe, and as Crime increaseth our Law-makers increase their Severity, to such a point that many modest Offences are deemed worthy of Punishment. This hath produced the strange Consequence, that many Magistrates and Juries are unwilling to convict petty Criminals, whose Guilt is manifest and proven, since they would then be taking away the precious Gift of Liberty. The Law is therefore held in Contempt by many Law-breakers. The Constables, whose Duty is it to seize the Criminals, are too few in number to detect or to deter any but the most feeble and imbecile; the Cause of their fewness being the English people's unwillingness to have any strong and central Force of Police, for Fear that this might abridge their antient Liberties.

In our *American* Plantations the State of Criminality is still more serious than in England, and, from what I hear, likely to grow even worse, if that were possible, in the Future. There almost every Person carryeth a Weapon, with which he will only too readily aid his Robberies, or accomplish the destruction of his Family, his Neighbours or his chief Rulers. There the Magistrates (some of whom are grossly and shamelessly corrupt) have so changed the Laws as to make it hard for the Constable to arrest, or Juries to convict-even the most notorious Thieves caught in the Act. There the Delays in the processes of Law and the Chicanery of the Lawyers (whereof I spake on another Occasion*) are even less supportable than in England and even more helpful to wrong-doing. After their Arrest the most hardened Criminals will be set free with the greatest of Ease, on payment of a small Sum of Yellow Metal, for the many Moons that may pass before their Trial; and many happily use this Period of Liberty to commit further Crimes. Nay more, there is a Species of Physicians called Head-Doctors, that will readily swear that a Malefactor on Trial is sick in his Brains, and therefore more fit to be sent to *Bedlam*† for remedial treatment than to the Gallows or the Prison-Hulks; and the Juries and Magistrates too often believe them. In the general Case, it is widely

* *Gulliver's Travels,* part iv.

† *Bedlam*: A lunatic asylum or madhouse. The word is a contraction of *Bethlehem,* St Mary of Bethlehem being the name of a religious house in London that was converted into a hospital for lunatics.

believed by the more liberal of the educated Sort, that *every* Malefactor is sick or mad, a suffering Victim of the Society on which he preys. Others are of the contrary Opinion, namely that in the present and future Condition of the Laws and of publick Opinion, he must be mad who does *not* commit Theft, so small is the Possibility of Detection, Arrest or Punishment, and so great the probable Profit that may ensue. . . . I was continuing in this Vein when I became aware that the Houyhnhnms were no longer listening, either because they were distracted by their many Anxieties or because they did not wish to hear what I had to say; and at length our Conversation broke off entirely when we heard a loud Commotion outside the Door.

Three Yahoos came slowly over the Fields and slouched up to the Hut of the New Master. The Houyhnhnms, who were gathering round, did not try to arrest them; and gradually ceased from their nervous Whinnying and watched them in curious Silence. I shuddered when I got my first sight of the Brutes since my Day on the Cliff; and I recognised the three Emissaries as belonging to the more active Band of the Wild Ones. I then saw the New Master for the first Time; I beheld a pale Horse, a well-fed, smooth-coated Member of the Nobility, who spoke with confident Eloquence, in an even Higher Voice than my recent Interlocutor; who now with his Friends joined him before the Stables. The Yahoos began to wave their Arms and gibber, making menacing and obscœne signs and Noises. The Master and his Colleagues were hard put to it, I could see, to make out their Meaning, until the Yahoos produced from behind their Backs pieces of Asses' Flesh and waved them in the Air. Shortly afterwards they broke off and withdrew to a nearby Coppice, where they sat scratching themselves. The Master at once sent round his Heralds to summon all the Houyhnhnms to an immediate Meeting of the Assembly; which I, by special Invitation of the Roan and the Chestnut, was privileged to attend.

The Master began by making a general Oration about Progress, Liberty and the Need for Compromise, which was greeted with no little Applause. When he had finished without saying anything about the recent Happenings, the Dapple-Grey asked him just what the Yahoos had been trying to say. The Master replied that the precise Meaning mattered not, but he felt that they had had a meaningful Dialogue. He then said that the Emissaries had made, he understood, one specific Demand, which he thought not unreasonable, requiring only that the Houyhnhnms hand over to them all their Asses. A Snort of Dismay went up from a large Section of the Assembly. A Speaker rose: he begged Leave to point out to the Right Honourable that since the number of working Yahoos was now greatly diminished, they were dependent on their Asses for most of the Work on the Land. Another speaker pointed out that the number of Asses was itself seriously reduced, because of the incessant Raids that the Yahoos had of late been carrying out; and that they could ill spare the few that remained. A third urged that they should concede some Part of this Demand, while they should make a full Inquiry into the Yahoos' Wishes in general and the Causes of the Present Discontents. Others replied that in Principle the Assembly should not give Way on this Occasion, since they would thereby be setting a Precedent for yielding to more expensive Demands in Future. The Debate proceeded keenly and with the usual Courtesy, until it seemed that some Compromise was about to be reached. At that point it was interrupted by a Foal, who galloped in and asked for Permission to speak; when this was granted, he announced that while the Debate had been in progress, several large Bands of Yahoos had rushed out of the Woods and carried off all the Asses that remained; there being none but himself and the other Foals to guard them, since all the adult Horses had been attending the Assembly. A Motion of Adjournment was then carried.

CHAPTER FIVE

Gulliver Among
the Young

*The Author's Doubts. The young Houyhnhnms. Their New
Stile of Poesy. Its Yahoo Characteristicks. The Decay of
Exercises. The Vices of London describ'd. The Envy of the
young Houyhnhnms thereat. Their Disregard of the antient
Laws. The Assembly in Permanent Session. The Yahoos'
Manner in Debate.*

DURING the next few Days nothing un-
toward happened; they were spent by many
Houyhnhnms in Doubt and Agony, apprais-
ing again their Attitudes and Philosophy. I too felt
the Need to reconsider my Thoughts: had I not
become, perhaps, too absolute in my Judgments, too
unsympathetic to the New Yahoos? Like most of my
Houyhnhnm Friends, I was of a Middle Age; surely
I must have much to learn from the Young, who
held the Future in their Hands. Accordingly I

sought out the Company of the Younger Set of Horses, no longer Foals or Yearlings, but not yet fully mature Stallions and Mares. I knew that I need not make any special Appointment with them, but that I would find the leading Spirits every Afternoon on the same Pasture, morosely standing around or occasionally dancing a few nervous Steps. They welcomed me, as before, with much Warmth, and expressed great Interest in all that concerned the Yahoo Kind. They asked me—which no Houyhnhnm had ever done before—what was the *English* for "Yahoo"; when I replied "Man", they addressed me as "h'man", towards the beginning of every Sentence throughout our Discourse. Their two great Topics of Conversation were Creation and Procreation, and on those important Items our subsequent Talk revolved. The leading Spirit among them was a Skewbald,* and to him I addressed my first Question: What did they mean by Creation?

"Creative Poetry, h'man," he replied. "You know, like making Words, Verses, all that kind of . . ."

I could not catch the last Word, nor could I comprehend much of his Speech, because of the strange mumbling Tone in which he delivered it, so unlike the clear Enunciation of his Elders. I soon saw that Skewbald was talking only of the New or Perfect Stile of Poesy, and had indeed very little Acquaintance with the antient Lore of Houyhnhnm

* In the manuscript the reading is "screwball", but since that is manifestly nonsense, I have amended the text to what Swift obviously intended.

Poetry; wherein the Justness of their Similes, and the Minuteness, as well as the Exactness of their Descriptions, are indeed inimitable. The Younger Set knew little about the traditional Epicks, beyond a few Formulae or Tags, such as "yahoo-taming Hyethon", "Swift-footed Cream" (illustrious Heroes of Legend) or "secure himself, he kicks out all around".* They had even less Knowledge of the antient Religion and Mythology of their People, being unable even to recite correctly the Eight Horses of the Sun, Effulgence, Fiery Red, No Loiterer, Thunder, Red Producer, Shining Like a Lamp, the Burning One, and Fiery Hot.† They scorned to learn the painful Craft of Verse-making, preferring the Spontaneous Over-Flow of their Feelings, even though they were but giving Vent, like the Æolists,‡ to Wind. They knew when they heard a good Line of Poetry (Skewbald added), because it infallibly gave them a strong Motion in the Gut.

When I hinted, begging his Pardon, that this was a somewhat Yahoo-like Criterion, since a Yahoo will rub his Belly not only when he has fed to Repletion but also when he undergoeth any strong Passion, he asked me brusquely what was wrong with that? The Yahoos had, in his Opinion, unsuspected Powers both as Criticks and as Poets. A savage Yahoo at the Head of his Tribe will harangue

* Cf. the horses of Hector, in Homer's *Iliad*, Ethon, Galathe, Podarge; and Horace, *Satires*, II. i. 20: "Recalcitrat undique tutus", which Swift quotes in *Gulliver's Travels*, Part IV, ch. 12.

† Cf. the horses of Helios, Acteon, Æthon, Amethea, Bronte, Erythreos, Lampos, Phlegon, Purocis.

‡ Aeolists: See Swift, *A Tale of a Tub*.

the multitude with more natural Eloquence and Gusto than all the Orators of the Houyhnhnm Assembly put together.* What were the Notes of Houyhnhnm Verse, coldly correct, to Yahoos' warbling wild?†

When I asked him, how could the Yahoos be said to produce Poesy, when they could only bawl, squeak or gibber, he replied that those Beings had the Root of the Matter in them, and that they had Musick in their *Souls*. When they would drum with their Fists on their inflated Chests, they produced a Symphony more agreeable than the over-refined Neighings of the established Bards.

Changing the Topick, I mentioned with Wonder the little Piles of Earth and Dung-smeared Slates that I had seen during my Day among the Wild Yahoos of the Valley; he explained that these Things were indeed Works of Art, and Nature scarcely methodiz'd; and even as he spoke, I could see another young Houyhnhnm scribble with his Hoof in a Patch of Sand, similar irregular Markings, save that some seemed to be crude Representations of a Mare's Private Parts. The admiring Onlookers cried out "Wild! Wild!", which was the most favoured Word of Commendation.

Returning to the more congenial Subject of Poesy, I said to the Skewbald that he had explained something of the *Stile* of the New Verses, but what of the *Content*? For I remembered that the Old

* For a similar expression, cf. Hugh Blair (1718–1800); preface to James MacPherson's *Ossian*.

† Cf. Thomas Warton (1728–90), "The Enthusiast".

Verses usually contained "either some Exalted Notions of Friendship and Benevolence, or the Praises of those who were Victors in Races, and other bodily Exercises".

"Copulation, h'man, pure Copulation," he answered, "that is all we sing"; and he went on to quote, by way of Illustration, a long Poem, which described in minute Detail how Stallions leapt on their Mares in Spring, in divers Positions; which, since it was not only outrageous but infinitely tedious, I shall forbear from translating for the Reader's Delectation.

I turned now to a horse of a different Colour, his Friend the Piebald, a fat Pony whose Mane fell to his Pasterns in greasy Ringlets. I asked him about the Athletic Contests, wherein the Youth of certain Districts meet to shew their Proficiency in Running, and Leaping, and other Feats of Strength or Agility. The Piebald answered that there were still a few Groups of Houyhnhnm Youth, who had formed fraternal Societies, and took Part in Racing; but neither he nor his Comrades cared much for such Pursuits, considering them childish as well as fatiguing. At most they could remember some of the names of the antient Winners, who had in former Times won the Palms, the Oaks and the Bays; and sometimes in Winter they would go to watch the more Hardy Colts sliding upon the Ice. But for the Rest he found neither Profit nor Delight in any form of Exercise, save one only.

The young Houyhnhnms shewed much Interest in the Yahoos of *Europe*, and pressed me to tell something of them, since they had received only brief, and, they suspected, prejudiced Accounts from their Sires and Dams. Upon this invitation, I began to speak about Life in the great Cities and in particular that of *London*. I repeated the Substance of what I had said about *Crime* to the Chestnut, and enlarged on other aspects of London, the Great Wen. I spoke first of the huge Number of Persons crammed into a small Plot of Land, Half a Million Souls and more; of the immense Throngs of driven Cattle, Wagons drawn by Oxen, Carriages by Houyhnhnms, Chairs carried by Irish Yahoos, and Citizens walking on their Hinder Legs, that croud the narrow Streets, so that often all Movement must cease and the Air be poisoned by the noisome Effluvia of the passers-by; which Air is further dirtied by the Sulphur and Soot from thousands of Fires of Sea-Coal. When the Wagons are able to move, many Citizens are perforce crushed to Death beneath the Wheels; to avoid which they will jostle one another against the Walls, thus occasioning much Trampling of Feet, Anger, Brawls, Beatings by drunken Bullies, and private Fights with Swords. In the middle of the Streets and in waste Places the House-holders discharge their Orts and Rubbidge, empty Bottles, waste Paper, Husks and decaying Vegetables; when it raineth, Sweepings from Butchers' Stalls, Dung, Guts, and Blood, Drown'd Puppies, stinking Sprats, all drench'd in Mud, Dead Cats and Turnip-Tops come tumbling down the Flood.*

The poorer Sort live in Huts and Stables many

* Jonathan Swift, *A Description of a City Shower*, October 1710.

Stories high, often with a whole Family pressed into one small Compartment; these Tenements are filthy and of a rickety Construction; here falling Houses thunder on your Head,* and there they catch Fire, trapping the wretched Inhabitants. Many Persons die of Diseases, caused by Fleas, Rats and dirty Water. In my Youth there was a Plague of Buboes that carried off a great Part of the Citizens, but we suffer also from other Sicknesses, as the Flux, the Jail Fever, and the *Cholera Morbus*. It hath been said that there is no second Generation of Londoners: their Offspring are all destroyed by Disease, and their Place taken by healthier Incomers from the Country Districts. These Plagues, though horrible in themselves, are yet providential; for if the Physicians succeeded in preventing and curing them, the Numbers of City-dwellers would soon rise beyond all endurable Bounds.

To ease their Miseries, the People drink greatly of a Liquor, which resembleth the Juice of the Yahoos' Root, but much stronger and more dire in its Effects, though agreeably flavoured with the Berry of the Juniper-Bush, and very cheap. To get enough of this Juice to attain Insensibility, the poorer Sort will sell or *pawn* all they possess. After drinking they will ryot bloodily, fall into a Stupour, dress in Rags, neglect their Children, become infected with open Sores, or starve to Death.† They

* "Here falling Houses thunder on your Head,
 And there a Rebel Student talks you dead."
Samuel Johnson, *London*, 1738. Although it is known that Pope admired this poem, this is the first proof that Swift had read it too.
 † See the celebrated engraving by William Hogarth, *Gin Lane*.

also use the Concoction of a Poppy-flower, either taken by itself or mixed with the Liquor, by which they are able to sleep throughout their Days of Rest.

This crouding together in narrow Dwellings and Alley-ways doth much inflame the carnal Desires of the City-dwellers; to supply which Needs there are great numbers of Persons called *Whores*, usually of the Female Sex; most had acquired a certain Malady, which breeds a Rottenness in the Bones of those who fall into their Embraces. An innocent girl-Yahoo will come to London from the Country, and fall into the clutches of a *Bawd* and a *Lecher*; she will become the *Mistress* of a rich *Protector*, but deceiving him for a young *Lover* will be driven out; next she will become the *Doxy* of a Criminal and of his Mates, be apprehended by a Magistrate and sent to *Bridewell* Prison, to beat Hemp; at length she will sink to extream Poverty, and expire of her *Venereal* Complaint, while the Doctors are quarrelling, her *Funeral* attended only by drunken and indifferent *Mourners*.*

I was at some Pains to explain each of the peculiar English Terms that I had used in this typical History, since I could see that my Audience was keenly interested. I went on with my Catalogue of the Miseries of City Life; listing Corruption in high Places; the frequent striking-off Work by those whose Duty it was to provide such publick Services as cleaning the Streets; the Brawling in the Schools,

---

* See William Hogarth, *The Harlot's Progress* (1731), a series of paintings, engravings of which he distributed the following year by subscription.

even by the youngest Yahoos; the Beggars and Abraham-men; the molesting of defenceless Females by randy Bucks and Rakes; the abject Poverty and Venality of the Authours of Grub-Street; the senseless destruction of publick and Private Property by Night-prowlers and Roaring Boys; and the creeping Insanity that by Degrees infects all that are huddled into the City, and at length must turn it into one great *Bedlam*-Hospital.

When I had finished I received much Applause from my Listeners, whereupon I asked them what they now thought about Life in the City.

They replied, "Dear Yahoo, we think it all exceeding wonderful, especially that part about Prostitution. It is our general Will to build just such a populous City here, on this Island; with Stables a Mile high and every other Amenity that thou hast spoken of. Wilt thou not stay with us and help us to build the New City? Verily thou seemest to be Gift of Providence, sent to our Shores to instruct us in the Great Society of the Future, and we have learned not to look a Gift-Yahoo in the Mouth."

No little taken aback, I asked them if in their Desire to create such a New City, they intended to violate the antient and strict Laws and Customs that had been framed for the purpose of controlling the Population of the Houyhnhnms? And here I may remind the Reader of the Terms in which those Customs had been explained to me: "When the Matron Houyhnhnms have produced one of each Sex, they no longer accompany with their Consorts, except they lose one of their Issue by some Casualty,

66

which very seldom happens: But in such a Case they meet again; or when the like Accident befalls a Person, whose Wife is past bearing, some other Couple bestows on him one of their own Colts, and then go together a second Time, until the Mother be pregnant. *This Caution is necessary to prevent the Country from being overburdened with Numbers.*"

When I repeated those Words to the Younger Houyhnhnms, they laughed, and said they would indeed sweep aside such fly-blown Ordinances; for they intended to marry as young as were possible, and to procreate their kind such with Vigour, that the Island would soon be stocked with multitudes of Foals of their own Breed. I argued that many of the Evils of the Wild Yahoos, that I had seen at the other End of the Island, were probably due to Force of Numbers; not only their Hunger, but the disgusting Practices in which they indulged, whereof I gave a brief Description. At this point, the civil Welcome of my Audience changed to cold Hostility; the Skewbald answered contemptuously that my Account of the Wild Yahoos was much exaggerated, and based on Misunderstanding and Prejudice. For instance, I had spoken slightingly of their eating of the Herb *Cannabis*; but this Herb was certainly harmless, or if it did dispose them to a certain Degree of Idleness, the Yahoos had (the speaker felt) every Right to a little Idleness, after the many Years of Hard Labour to which their Houyhnhnm Masters had condemn'd them. "No, we younger People think that we have much to learn from the Yahoos; as in the Field of Art, so in the

Fields of Procreation and Politics, they have a Message for us." This was greeted with Applause; for my Part, I did not yet grasp the Significance of his last Words.

At that moment the Heralds began to summon all the Houyhnhnms to yet another Meeting of the Assembly. The younger Set cantered off to the Meeting-place in high Spirits, and I followed as quickly as I might. The Motion before the Houses was as follows: that the Assembly should be held every Day. This was proposed by the Chestnut, who argued, with some Show of Logick, that since special Meetings were being called with increasing Frequency, in these critical Times, it would be more reasonable to keep the Assembly in permanent Session, with Adjournments from Time to Time; and seconded by the Skewbald, who urged that every Matter of *Concern* to them all, and especially their Dealings with the Yahoos, should be kept under continual Review, and discussed by every Member of the Community; he was cheered by his young Comrades. Opposing the Motion, the Dapple-Grey objected that such daily Meetings would leave little Time for any other Work, and in View of the Depletion of their Asses and Working Yahoos, they could ill afford to neglect their Cattle and Crops by spending Hours every Day in Committee. The Debate continued, with much being said on both Sides, when suddenly some fifty Yahoos rushed into the Meeting-Place and squatted on the Ground. The Dapple-Grey at once asked the Master, who was in the Chair, to have the Ushers eject them; he replied that he considered such Action to fall outside his Prerogative, and requested that the Matter be put to a Vote. By a Small Minority it was resolved that the Yahoos be allowed to remain until the End of the Session. The Master said that he welcomed this Decision, since it would give the Yahoos an Opportunity to be educated in the Procedures of the Assembly.

When the Debate was resumed on the first Question, the Yahoos took an increasingly active Part in the Proceedings. They crudely imitated the oratorical Gestures of the Speakers, as when one would raise a Hoof to the Sky, or lay it across his Heart. They raised Shrieks of Applause, shaking their clenched Fists, when the Piebald spoke in Denunciation of the rigid and out-moded Customs of the Assembly; and when Iron-Grey, a friend of the Dapple-Grey's, tried to make a speech in defence of Tradition and the Laws of Reason, they howled him down, drumming on their Chests until he could no longer be heard, and even trying to lay their Paws on him. It soon became apparent that there was no longer any Freedom of Speech for any but the more extream of the Houyhnhnms, so loudly did the Yahoos intervene, grunting "Ut, Ut, Ut," hissing, making lascivious Gestures and throwing Showers of Dirt. I could not understand how it was that the Brutes, who had neither Speech nor the Understanding of Speech, could know which Orators to cheer and which to objurgate, until I saw the Skewbald making secret Signs behind his Back to prompt them; waving in the Air what I took to be small bundles of fragrant, or bitter Herbs, that their keen Muzzles could not fail to snuff, at the appropriate Moments. Suddenly the Brutes got up in a Body and scrambled out, leaving their customary Tokens behind them on the Ground. A Resolution was then put by the Chestnut to the Effect that the Yahoos be asked to send permanent Representatives to the Assembly; he felt that this Afternoon had been a remarkable Occasion for all of them, and that much Progress had been made towards mutual Understanding. This Motion was however defeated, and a substituted Resolution, that the Yahoos should be excluded from the Assembly, and punished if they should again intrude, was carried by a substantial Majority.

CHAPTER SIX

The Dapple-Grey: The Final Assembly

The Dapple-Grey admonisheth the Author. His Opinion of the young Houyhnhnms, and of the Chestnut, and of the other Houyhnhnms. The Polity of the New Master. The Final Assembly. The Yahoos invade the Podium. They invite the Houyhnhnms to eat Dirt and terrify them with Fires. The Rout of the Houyhnhnms.

A LITTLE later, in the Middle of the Night, I was summoned to the Presence of the Dapple-Grey, who had played so notable a part in the latest Assembly. One of his Clansmen escorted me in Silence to his Stables, which were removed at a Distance of some Miles, in a lonely Countryside. He received me seated, in his plain but well-built Stall lit by one Rush-Light.

"Yahoo," he began sternly, "it will not have escaped thy attention that I was displeased to see thee return to the Island. Indeed, I believed that thou hadst returned many Moons earlier, had been using thy Rudiments of Reason to stir up the Yahoos of the Mountains to Mischief, and wert entering our Village as a Spy, to ensnare the more foolish of our People. I now find myself to have been mistaken in this Opinion; and indeed it hath been reported to me on good Authority that thou, though but a meer Yahoo by Origin, hast a little good Sense in thee, and hast not been deceived by *the Thing that is not.*" Thereon, extending his Hoof, he suffered me to lift it to my Mouth.

Before I report our Discourse on that Night, I must first attempt to describe the Character of the Dapple-Grey. Born into one of the noblest Strains of the Island, he had been in his Youth a notable Athlete; often a Victor in the Games and receiving many a Song made in his Praise. He had also been remarkably Proficient in those Military Exercises that the Houyhnhnms, though they have never been invaded, deem necessary for the Defence of their Island. He was a distinguished Poet, if not quite of the first Rank; but had won more Fame for his exhaustive Knowledge of the antient Odes and Epicks. If I were asked which non-Houyhnhnm I should compare him to, I should chuse my Lord Munodi, of Balnibarbi, whom I have described in the Third Book of my *Travels*: like my Lord, the Dapple-Grey was a Country Gentleman of the more enlightened Sort, a great Improver of his Estate, yet as much at Home in the Affairs of the Assembly as among his Ploughs and Harrows. Somewhat stiff in his joints and grizzled with Age, he was still a formidable Runner and of a handsome Presence. Soldier, Scholar, Horse of Horses, he cast a cold Eye on Life and Death. He possessed all the Points and Virtues most prized in his People, and of these I should single out for Praise his Courage and Generosity. The Dapple-Grey and a few of his Clansmen and Friends were the last of the Houyhnhnms that held to the grand Maxim of their Ancestors: "to cultivate *Reason*, and to be wholly governed by it". By *Reason*, I mean that which strikes with immediate Conviction, "as it needs must do," my Old Master would say, "where it is not mingled, obscured or discoloured by Passion and Interest".

In recording the Dapple-Grey's Conversation, I have found one great Difficulty: namely, of rendering, in *English*, the singular Purity of his Style. Clear, masculine and smooth, it was in compleat Contrast to the strange, new-fangl'd Jargon and Sentimental Rhetorick of the Chestnut, Skewbald and Piebald. My noble Friend (as henceforward I dare call him) had formed his Style both on the Natural Speech of Rural Simplicity, and on the best Authours, antient and modern. I despair of translating his Discourse with Felicity, and beg the Reader's Forbearance.

We first discussed the political Events of the past few Days, and the Debates in the Assembly. I rejoiced in the new-found Strength of the Majority, and in their firm Decision to exclude the Yahoos from their Councils.

"My good Yahoo," he replied, "do not be

73

deceived. The Strength of the Majority is but an outward Show; the Master and his Friends are waiting for the Occasion to sway the Assembly in the other Direction, and I am sure that within a few Days they will have their Will."

When I expressed Astonishment at this, he answered that evidently I had not understood the Degree of Corruption that had entered into the Hearts of his Fellows, and how they had acquired the Habit of Vacillating and Facing Both Ways.

I asked if he thought that the Rage of the Yahoos had somewhat abated, and that the stauncher Party of the Houyhnhnms might not now have won a Respite in which to rally their Forces.

"No (he said), on the Contrary, the unheard-of Audacity of the Brutes increaseth daily, as doth the Negligence of their sometime Masters. A few Nights ago, they went so far as to steal a young Foal out of the Stables, which had been carelessly left unguarded. The Stable Doors were immediately bolted, but the poor Foal was never rescued, and indeed met with a dismal Fate. On the next Day a Scout reported that he had seen a Gang of Yahoos standing around the Foal's Corpse, flogging it in the Manner of a Ceremony, so as to leave no Doubt as to their Intention of doing likewise to our entire Stock. I am certain that they are plotting further Mischief, but what form this will take I know not; my capacity for Prophecy is exhausted. But I am sure that the Master and his Colleagues will be indisposed to meet the next Assault with Firmness. As for our own Party, we are but few; and have lost much of our former

Authority, which was founded on Reason and on Reason alone. But we shall fight to the End; our Mettle will grow the more, as our Might lessens."*

Turning from recent Affairs to the more philosophical Principles that underlay the Dissensions, I asked him for Information about the various Sorts and Conditions of the New Yahoos, that I had seen in the Mountains. . .†

*   *   *   *   *

DAPPLE-GREY: "Although there be some among the younger Breed—I hope it will not seem immodest if I name my own Colt and Filly—who are true to the old Ways, many of them, like those you spoke, are Scoundrels, or Imbeciles. And, as you have observed, the worst are those who profess the Art of Poesy. For this I much blame their Dams and Sires, who have failed to enjoyn to them the Lessons of *Temperance, Industry, Exercise* and *Cleanliness*; but have permitted them to grow up in Idleness and Luxury. Thou hast heard them speak of the Herb *Cannabis*; but didst thou know that they go into the Yahoo Region of the Island to eat of this Herb,

* Probably yet another quotation from the ancient epic poetry of the Houyhnhnms.

† Here there is an hiatus in the manuscript. It looks as if Swift tore out a whole page at this point. I conjecture that he feared the censorship of the Whigs, who were anticipating the Jacobite invasion of the following year; or possibly, given the liberal and progressive climate of opinion that existed in the mid-1740s, Swift felt that anything he wrote on this subject would be totally misunderstood.

though that is expressly forbidden by an Exhortation of the Assembly? And some—horrible to relate—have criminal Intercourse with young Yahoos, of both Sexes; falling into the Sleep of Reason, they beget Monsters. As to their Politicks, they talk much of Reform, but in their Hearts they intend, as they will sometimes admit, the Destruction of our Institutions; which would also be the Goal of the active Yahoos (could these but comprehend that they had a Goal). What they will set up in the place of our established Polity, they know not; but hope that out of Chaos there will arise the New Horse. To compass their Ends, they will lend support with their Tongues to the most violent Deeds of the New Yahoos.'

I asked for the Truth about Chestnut and his Friends.

DAPPLE GREY: "They have given up the Horse-Sense of their Ancestors, for the New Sensibility; and have traded Reason, for what they falsely interpret as Nature. I remember well the first Time that Chestnut said in the Assembly that, after all, there was something more *Natural* about the Yahoos, something more gay and spontaneous (but I scorn to reproduce his sentimental Bombast further). I replied, 'Don't cant to me about Savages, Sir! The Life of the Yahoos is nasty, brutish and short; they are incapable of drawing up that first Contract of Civil Society, which ensures personal Safety and Freedom of Speech. Since that is *the Thing which is*, we have nothing to learn from them.' You will forgive my quoting my own Words, which I do, not

76

out of Self-Conceit, but because they put the Case of our Party most clearly. It is the Duty of a Houyhnhnm to rid his Mind of all the Passions, of which the most degrading is Fear. But the Mind of Chestnut is clouded with the Passions of Fear, Guilt, Doubt, and the Desire to be flattered by the Young. I count him but a vain Thing."

What of my kindly Host, the Roan?

DAPPLE GREY: "He is confused, poor Fellow."

And what of the Sorrel Nag?

DAPPLE GREY: "The Servant Class, to which the worthy Sorrel Nag belongs, and which is solely concerned with Farming, is on the Whole ill-disposed towards the new Turn in our Affairs. But it is passive, and cannot be counted on in the dire Straits that we are entering."

I then asked him to give me the Character of the New Master, who had played, and would play, a critical Part in the Proceedings.

DAPPLE GREY: "The Master is a Noble-horse of high Abilities and extensive Benevolence. He is also devious in his Counsels, and weak in his Decisions. His Birth and Upbringing were singular and may explain something of his Character. You will recall that of all the Practices of the Yahoos of your Land, which you related seven Years ago, none raised more Resentment among us than the Manner and Use of *Castrating* Horses among you, to hinder them from propagating their Kind, and to render them more servile. Now, you must learn that, by the Vicissitudes of Chance, one in ten thousand Colts in our Land is foaled *without Stones*, a Gelding from his

77

Birth. This Deviation from what is fit and proper in Nature causeth us such Horrour, that by Custom we used to expose the new-born Foal on a lonely Hillside. The New Master's was such a Condition, and as an Infant he was duly exposed. But he was rescued by a kindly Herd-horse, who brought him up in Secret, as his own Colt. The Youth thrived and joined the other Colts in Training, where he showed singular Talents. When he had attained to adult Years, the Flaw in his bodily Constitution was discovered and made publick; but by that Time our People had turned against what they now held to be the harsh Custom of their Ancestors, and he was suffered to live. Besides, the Youth had shown such skill in the managing of Affairs that he was now considered to be indispensable; and in due course of Time was chosen to be the sole Master of our People.

"I for one did not approve of placing so much Power in the Hooves of one Houyhnhnm. I have ever been opposed to tyrannick Government by One Ruler, as I have been opposed to Government by the Many, the hundred-headed Rabble; I believe in Government by the Few.* Antiently the Power of counselling (and antiently to counsel was to rule) was shared between the Heads of every Household, who were the wisest Elders; and the Representative Assembly of the whole Nation met only every fourth

* This corresponds to Swift's own views on the Art of Government. Cf. *A Discourse on the Contests and Dissensions in Athens and Rome* (1701), written with reference to the impeachment of the Whig Lords.

Year, at the Vernal Equinox. But now we have a sole Ruler, who makes, without consulting the Elders, decisions of grave Import; and yet from Time to Time is shaken like a Reed by the Winds that blow from the frequent Assemblies.

"The Master, then, is likely to yield to any Pressure exerted on him by the various Parties in the Assembly, by the younger Set of Houyhnhnms (who meet also outside the Assembly) and by the Yahoos. But you must not think that he is meerly a Weakling, or that to yield is unwelcome to him. It is not: he sincerely desireth Change in our Polity, and will gladly go along the Path that the Chestnut and his Friends have pointed out to you. The Chestnut, indeed, is his Intimate and Spokesman. The Master and this *Cabal* consider that the Majority of the Assembly is still too stiff-necked, set in its Ways, and resistant to Change; and to the End of breaking the Spirit of the Assembly, they are ready to use the most dubious Means. They have not scrupled to encourage the Young to rail against their Elders and Betters; and have even used the Threat of Yahoo Power to frighten or to confuse the uncertain and hesitant Part of the Assembly. Nay, it hath been reported to me by a Friend (who could never say *the Thing which is not*) that the Master and the Chestnut have had privy Dealings with certain active Yahoos, bribing them with Asses' Flesh and shining Stones to stay, or to renew, their Demands, as the Situation has required. I doubt not that the Master wishes the Yahoos to send Representatives to the Assembly, although he hath not yet declared

79

his Wish in publick; or that he will do everything in his Power to make the Assembly reverse their last Exhortation. Therefore, be prepared for the worst."

After some further Discourse, concerning minuter Points of the Affairs of State (wherewith I shall not trouble the Reader), I turned to more philosophical Considerations. I asked him what he considered the great Business of Life. He replied, to practise Friendship and Benevolence; to labour honestly in the Fields; to train up the Young in Skill and Hardiness; and to uphold the antient Canons of the Poetick Art. In Politicks, he cherished the grand Principle of Subordination, now almost forgot; the maintaining of Law and Order; the prevention of any Increase in the Population; and the guiding of all Affairs by Reason, and by Reason alone. He ended by paying me the Compliment of repeating Words from a Yahoo's Mouth, that I had quoted to him: he agreed fervently with the King of Brobdingnag, that "whoever could make two Ears of Corn, or two Blades of Grass grow upon a Spot of Ground where only one grew before; would deserve better of Mankind, and do more essential Service to his Country, than the whole Race of Politicians put together".

The Day came for the Assembly to meet again; and again I attended as an Observer. The Proceedings opened with the Master in the Chair. He made a Speech about the Mutability of all mortal Things, the Need for Change, and the Progress of Poesy. I could not see that this was germane to the Situation facing the Assembly, but doubtless it was intended to prepare the Members' Minds for what was to come.

His Words were received with some Applause. He then gave the Speaker's Wand to the Chestnut, who made the direct Proposal that the Assembly should reverse its last Decision, *viz.* that the Yahoos should not be permitted to send Representatives to this Body, and that those who forcibly insisted on doing so, should be punished. He argued, with much Eloquence, that not only were they forced to upset their former Resolution by the Menaces of the Yahoos (which were growing daily more desperate), but on the Grounds of Reason, as well as of Sentiment, this seemed to him the noblest Course to pursue. The Yahoos resented even the Threat of Punishment, and was he to say that their Resentment was unjustified? As for their sending Representatives, the Assembly (he felt) would be the richer in collective Wisdom from the Contributions that those People had to offer.

He was answered by the Dapple-Grey on the expected Lines, and the Debate continued with some Warmth; when I happened to turn my Gaze away from the Speakers, and saw with Horrour that the Place of Assembly was wholly surrounded by Yahoos, a Circumstance that had passed unnoticed by the Houyhnhnms, so intent had they been on the Debate. In the Van were the fifty-odd Yahoo Leaders, now holding rude Clubs made from Branches and shaking them in the Air; some were even riding, I observed with Dismay, on the Asses that they had stolen from their Masters. Behind them, a Sight even more astonishing, was gathered the entire, or almost the entire, Body of Yahoos of the Island: they were squatting on the Ground, in Silence and peacably enough, save that they were quivering, and slavering at their Muzzles, in Anticipation of the Outcome. The Members of the Assembly now became aware of what was happening, and the Tone of the Debate changed sharply. The Skewbald and the Piebald, speaking for the younger Set, now threatened to seize and occupy the principal Stables, in imitation of the Yahoos' famous Action, unless the Assembly forthwith rescinded its previous Decision; whereupon the Yahoo Leaders set up a fearsome Yelling, which was earnestly echoed by the entire Tribe. In this Situation it did not take the Assembly long to make up its collective Mind: the Chestnut's Motion was immediately carried, the Dapple-Grey and a few others making up the Minority. The fifty Yahoos were forthwith admitted as legal Representatives, and entered the Assembly.

This was the Occasion for much Self-Congratulation. Several Houyhnhnms arose to say that by their magnanimous Act they had without doubt avoided the Risk of Blood-shedding and the Employment of the *Bulls*; Speakers who had hitherto been on opposite Sides of the House now embraced, nuzzling one another in the Kiss of Peace. The Master threw his Legs around the Leading Spirits of the Yahoos, weeping Tears of Joy, notwithstanding that he was mocked by their satirick Mimicry of his Actions. The Chestnut was heard to say, above the general Hubbub, "Let us, brethren, run to the River and dip ourselves in the Waters thereof, to signify that we are beginning a New Life, and inaugurating the

New Commonwealth, and the Community of Yahoo and Houyhnhnm."—Such language as I had never before heard from a Horse's Mouth, but which resembled the Canting of our Æolists, Third-Monarchy Men, and other enthusiastick Sects of the English Yahoos.

The Yahoos' Representatives now proceeded to the Podium and began to address the first Session of the newly constituted Assembly. I observed that not only were they carrying Clubs, but that to the Tips of these they had fastened sharp Lumps of Flint. Some wore Bands around their Heads, in which they had stuck the Plumage of the *Gnayh* (a large Bird of Prey). I could see that the Education of the Yahoos, as advocated by the Chestnut, had proceeded apace, and that they were now well on the Road from Savagery to the Barbarick Condition. Given an attentive Hearing, they began to address the Assembly, which they did as a Chorus. It was by no means clear to the Houyhnhnms, at first, what their Posturings, Voidings of Excrement and Urine, Slobberings and Barkings were intended to signify; although evidently they were making a new *Demand*. The Meaning first became plain to the younger Houyhnhnm Caucus, used, as they were, to Intercourse with the Orators; and soon I too, having an innate Knowledge of the Brutes' Gestures, could translate the Ideas as: "Be like us! Be Yahoos! Roll in the Dirt! Eat Dirt!" When the younger Set began to illustrate this Meaning, by vigorously performing the required Actions, of rolling and eating, to the Applause of the Yahoos, the Import of the Demand was presently comprehended by even the weakest Noddle in the Assembly. Many of the Houyhnhnms showed an understandable Reluctance to comply, and it looked for a while likely that there would be a general Resistance, led by Dapple-Grey and his Party.

To explain how this Reluctance was overcome, I must make a short Digression concerning Fire. Of the four Elements of Nature, Fire is the one for which the Houyhnhnm have the least Liking. They use it in Moderation, in their Huts, for the boiling of Oats and the like, but always taking the greatest Precautions against Accidents. When Lightning strikes an Oak Tree, causing it to burst into Flame, or when during the dry Season, which happens but rarely, some Parts of the Forests are set alight, the Houyhnhnms are inwardly perturbed. Though a naturally brave People, and schooled in the Mastery of their Passions, they will on such Occasions shew a few outward Signs of Fear, in their trembling and sweating, until the Danger be past.

At this critical Moment, I perceived that some of the leading Yahoos were lighting Fires, of dry Twigs and Rosin. I wondered greatly how the Brutes had learned to do this, since they had previously had no Knowledge of this important Art; until I discovered to my Mortification that I no longer possessed my spare Flint-and-Tinder-Box in my Breeches Pocket. I had no doubt dropped it carelessly, perhaps during my Journey through the Forest; and a Yahoo must have picked it up and by Accident discovered its Use. The Appearance of the Fires was too much for the over-wrought Houyhnhnms. They broke Ranks, running in all Directions, rearing up, whinnying piteously, their nostrils flaring.

The Dusk was now beginning to fall, and in the Light of the Bon-fires the Skins of the Yahoos took on the Hue of Copper. They began to pursue the Horses, trying to throw round their Necks Loops of Rope, that they had made from Creepers; and when this proved difficult, they seized their Victims' Manes, and leapt on their Backs, uttering wild Whoops. The Dapple-Grey and his Friends put up a spirited Fight, kicking out with Skill and Mettle, but they were soon out-number'd. Judging further Resistance to be in Vain, they collected themselves together in a small Troop; then acting in Concert, they broke through the surrounding Ring of their Enemies, and gallop'd towards the Sea-shoar. The Dapple-Grey shouted to me as he swept past, "Take care of thyself, good Yahoo." And soon I saw them in the Distance plunge into the Sea and swim away. In the general Turmoil, I defended myself as best I could, suffering some Blows and Indignities, but without great Mishap. Then during a Lull in the Battle, I turned my Gaze to the Centre of the Assembly-Place, and there saw a singular Event: the Master, the Chestnut, and their Party were rolling in the Dirt and eating thereof, with evident Satisfaction, surrounded by a Mob of jeering Yahoos.

CHAPTER SEVEN

Conclusion

The Author defends himself. The Fate of the Sorrel Nag. The Author is borne away by the Dapple-Grey's Colt. He bids farewell to the Land of the Houyhnhnms. He puts to Sea. The Last of the Dapple-Grey. The Author's Escape. His present lamentable Condition.

T was now Time for me to think of my own Escape. I endeavoured to join the Sorrel Nag, who was at some Distance, still fighting bravely. Two Yahoos barred my Way; and I drew my Hanger to defend my self. These horrible Animals had the boldness to attack me on both Sides, and one of them held his Fore-feet at my Collar; but I had the good Fortune to rip up his Belly before he could do me any Mischief. He fell down at my Feet; and the other seeing the Fate of his Comrade, made his Escape, but not without one good Wound on the Back, which I gave him as he fled, and made the Blood run trickling from him.

86

When I reached the Sorrel Nag, he asked me to hold his Mane and jump on his Back; but he had not gone more than a few Steps, when he unluckily stumbl'd on a Mole-Hill and fell, throwing me to the Ground.* Before he could rise, a Band of Yahoos had seized him, sinking their Fangs and Claws into his Side; and I could not save my unfortunate Friend from Destruction.

I considered my Situation to be without Hope, when the Son of the Dapple-Grey galloped up to me. "Leap on my Back, gentle Yahoo," he said, "and I will carry thee to the Forest." Holding him so tight that I resembled a *Centaur*, I began my last thunderous Charge through the Ranks of the Yahoos. A hater of his Kind ran to the Wood of Madness, his Mane foaming in the Moon, his Eyeballs Stars: it was I.†

I was pursued by two more whooping Yahoos, mounted on swift and now compliant Chargers. When we were overtaken, I discharged my Pistol at one, who fell heavily into the Dust; and I dismounted the other with a Blow of my Hanger. We reached the Edge of the thick Forest, where no Horse could pass; and here I climb'd down, and embraced the Dapple-Grey's Colt. Weeping bitterly, he said, "Farewell, gentle Yahoo. For this Time have I saved thee, although the Day of Doom is near thee, nor shall we be the Cause thereof, but a mighty

* Sorrel, the horse of King William III, met with a similar accident in 1702.

† This sentence seems to have been added to the manuscript by a later hand.

god and overpowering Fate.* I go now to join my Father." And he cantered across the Plains towards the Sea-Shoar, until he was out of Sight.

I entered the thick Forest, cutting my Way with my Hanger through the Undergrowth, until I found an old Yahoo-Trail. I was at first in mortal Apprehension, until I recollected that there would be few, if any, Yahoos left in this Part of the Island, since the entire Body were presently engaged in subduing the Houyhnhnms. And so it turned out to be: I retraced my Steps without overmuch Difficulty to the Plain in the Valley, where I had spent my first Day. It was deserted, save for a few old or invalid Yahoos, gibbering softly to themselves in their Caves, who made no Attempt to molest me. On the Floor of the quadrangular Clearing, where there had formerly been a Throng of the Brutes, there was now only an immense Pile of Rubbidge: consisting of empty Gourds, strips of Bark, chewn Leaves of the Herb *Cannabis*, torn-out Hair and Scurf removed from their Bodies by Scratching. Even the appalling Stench had begun to dissipate itself, as a fresh Breeze blew up the Gorge from the Sea. I entered the Gorge, passing the Cliff where I had spent my first Day, and made my Way past the Water-Falls. My temper is not very susceptible of Enthusiasm, but I confess that I found this a most beautiful Country; neither do I remember to have seen a more delightful Prospect.

* An apt quotation from another of the Houyhnhnm epics: cf. Homer, *Iliad*, xix, 408–10, where the horse Xanthos addresses Achilles.

At the Foot of the Gorge, I found my Boat in the Sea-Cave where I had left it, undiscover'd by the Yahoos; I inspected the Sail, Oars, and Store of Provisions, which were all in good Condition, and filled my Water-bottles. I rowl'd the Boat over the Shingle, set up Sail, and set my Course by Compass in the direction of *New-Holland*.

Unluckily the Current once again prov'd too strong for my Sail and Oars, and carried me straight out into the Ocean, about ninety Degrees off Course. When I was some Miles away from the Island, which was yet clearly visible, I saw my old Mentor the Dapple-Grey swimming in the Waves. With Expedition I row'd toward him, and coming alongside tried to hoist him into the Boat. But it proved impossible to lift a heavy Stallion into a small Boat, and, besides, he was already greatly weaken'd. After my Efforts had prov'd in vain, he shook his Head proudly; and snorting, "Tell the World, Gentle Yahoo, tell the World!" he sank beneath the Surface. Now I saw only the wild white Horses, as our Mariners call them.

The following Night was dark, the Sky much obscur'd with Clouds. In the far Distance, on a Bearing which I took to be that of *New-Holland*, I saw a very bright Light; and a little later a burning Object move rapidly over the Sky, although it was too cloudy for me to follow its celestial Motion exactly. Over the Island of the Houyhnhnm, which was then beneath the Horizon, I saw a violent Flame, and heard a loud Clap, as of Thunder. But whether these Phænomena were volcanic Eruptions (which have been commonly reported by Travellers in these Latitudes), or occasioned by the Fall of a Meteor or a Comet, I could not determine. On the next Morning, I could perceive with my Perspective Glass nothing in the Direction of the Island, save only a faint Smoak rising in the Air.

After many Days, when my Provisions had given out, I was pick'd up by the *Adventure*, a stout Ship of three Hundred Tuns, Capt. John Trelawney, a *Cornish* man, Commander. I shall not trouble the Reader with a particular Account of this Voyage; which, indeed, since I was more dead than alive, I remember little about. When we arrived at Falmouth, I was still grievously ill with the Scurvy, and have never recovered my Health to this Day.

When I returned to my House at *Newark* (whither I had removed from *Redriff*), my Condition was even less happy than before. I had long ago lost all my Yahoo Friends, save only Captain Mendez; about whose Safety I made extensive Inquiries. At length I learnt that he had not returned from his last Voyage. From the Appearance of one of his Crew, who had been picked up dead near *New-Holland*, it had been conjectured that there had been some Kind of Explosion in his Ship, but this could not be established with Certitude. I grieved much for my Friend, the most civil Yahoo I had known, and bewailed that I might have provided the Occasion for his untimely Death. My Wife and my Children now found my Gloom and Spleen so impossible to tolerate, that they left my House for ever.

At length I could no longer suffer even the

Company of my Horses; their Conversation was more tedious than before, and, besides, I suspected them of Treachery. Finally, when I had lost all my Money, I sold them; but continued to live in the deserted Stables, still savouring with a little Pleasure the Smell of Straw and Horse-dung. My Withers began to give way, and I developed Galls from rubbing my Back on an old Scratching-Post. I no longer stiled myself Lemuel Gulliver, first a Surgeon, and then a Captain of several Ships; but I have called my name Nagg, in commemoration of my lamented Friend, the Sorrel Nag. I have crept into a Bin, that formerly held Oats, and have pulled the Cover over my Head; and now I sit in the Dark, scribbling, scribbling...

FINIS